Dear Parent:

Congratulations! Your child is taking the first steps on an exciting journey. The destination? Independent reading!

STEP INTO READING® will help your child get there. The program offers five steps to reading success. Each step includes fun stories and colorful art. There are also Step into Reading Sticker Books, Step into Reading Math Readers, Step into Reading Write-In Readers, Step into Reading Phonics Readers, and Step into Reading Phonics First Steps! Boxed Sets—a complete literacy program with something for every child.

Learning to Read, Step by Step!

Ready to Read Preschool–Kindergarten
• big type and easy words • rhyme and rhythm • picture clues
For children who know the alphabet and are eager to begin reading.

Reading with Help Preschool–Grade 1
• basic vocabulary • short sentences • simple stories
For children who recognize familiar words and sound out new words with help.

Reading on Your Own Grades 1–3
• engaging characters • easy-to-follow plots • popular topics
For children who are ready to read on their own.

Reading Paragraphs Grades 2–3
• challenging vocabulary • short paragraphs • exciting stories
For newly independent readers who read simple sentences with confidence.

Ready for Chapters Grades 2–4
• chapters • longer paragraphs • full-color art
For children who want to take the plunge into chapter books but still like colorful pictures.

STEP INTO READING® is designed to give every child a successful reading experience. The grade levels are only guides. Children can progress through the steps at their own speed, developing confidence in their reading, no matter what their grade.

Remember, a lifetime love of reading starts with a single step!

For Tanya, because she loves bunnies
—T.R.

Copyright © 2010 Disney Enterprises, Inc. All rights reserved. Published in the United States by Random House Children's Books, a division of Random House, Inc., 1745 Broadway, New York, NY 10019, and in Canada by Random House of Canada Limited, Toronto, in conjunction with Disney Enterprises, Inc.

Step into Reading, Random House, and the Random House colophon are registered trademarks of Random House, Inc.

Visit us on the Web!
www.stepintoreading.com
www.randomhouse.com/kids

Educators and librarians, for a variety of teaching tools, visit us at
www.randomhouse.com/teachers

Library of Congress Cataloging-in-Publication Data

Redbank, Tennant.
Beck's bunny secret / by Tennant Redbank ; [illustrated by Disney Storybook Artists].
p. cm. — (Step into reading. Step 3 book)
"Fairies."
ISBN 978-0-7364-2643-5 (trade) — ISBN 978-0-7364-8075-8 (lib. bdg.)
I. Disney Storybook Artists. II. Title.
PZ7.R24455Be 2010 [E]—dc22 2009012207

Printed in the United States of America   10 9 8 7 6 5 4 3 2 1

STEP INTO READING®

STEP 3

Beck's Bunny Secret

By Tennant Redbank

Illustrated by Denise Shimabukuro
and the Disney Storybook Artists

Random House 🏠 New York

Beck looked to her right.

She looked to her left.

She looked behind her.

Then she smiled.

She was alone.

She parted the blades
in a clump of grass
and slipped inside.

Beck had a secret.

It was a very fuzzy secret.

It was a baby bunny named Bitty.

Beck was taking care of him.

"I can't let anyone

know you are here,"

Beck said to Bitty.

She stroked his soft ears.

"Especially Fawn."

Fawn always teased Beck

about her baby animals.

This wasn't the only time

Beck had helped a stray animal.

First there was the baby skunk.

P-U!

Rosetta was mad at her

for ages after that.

Then there was

the baby warty toad.

He was very cute.

But he made Beck's skin

all bumpy.

The worst was the egg

Beck found in Brackle Swamp.

She didn't know

it was a crocodile egg!

Fawn always scolded
Beck about the baby animals.
Beck didn't want
to get in trouble.
Beck stroked Bitty's soft fur.
"But you're so cute!" she said.
Suddenly, she heard a voice.

"Beck! Where are you?"

Beck gasped.

It was Fawn!

"Shhh," Beck told Bitty.

Beck flew over to Fawn.

"There you are!"

Fawn said to Beck.

Rustle, rustle, rustle.

"What's that noise?"

Fawn asked.

Beck's face turned red.

Bitty must be hopping about!

Rustle, rustle, rustle.

Fawn pointed to Bitty's hiding spot.

"It's coming from

that clump of grass!" she cried.

Beck told Fawn it was
just the wind.
Fawn shook her head.
"I'm not a weather talent,"
she said.
"But even I can tell
there's no wind today."
Fawn flew over to the grass.

Beck covered her eyes.

Fawn parted the grass

and looked inside.

Beck peeked between her fingers.

There was nothing there.

Bitty was gone!

Beck dropped her hands.

"See? It was the wind,"

she said.

Fawn shrugged.

Then she flew off.

Right away,

Beck dove into the grass.

She searched high and low.

Bitty was not there.

Bitty was missing!

Beck had to find him.

Where would a baby bunny go?

Bunnies loved to eat.

Beck flew to the gardens.

She checked the lettuce patch.

Nothing.

Beck tried the carrot patch.

All the carrots were in order.

There was no sign of Bitty.

Beck looked at the peas . . .

and the beans . . .

and the beets.

No baby bunny had nibbled them.

Beck flew to the fairy-dust mill.

"Has anything been eating

your pumpkin shells?"

she asked Terence.

Terence shook his head.

Maybe Bitty wasn't hungry.

Maybe he was thirsty!

Beck flew to the stream.

Rani was making a leaf boat.

"Have you seen

any paw prints nearby?"

Beck asked

the water-talent fairy.

"No," Rani told her.

"But if I do, I'll let you know!"

Where could Bitty be?

Beck checked

Mother Dove's nest.

She checked Tinker Bell's workshop.

She dropped by Bess's art studio.

She stopped by Lily's garden.

She couldn't find Bitty anywhere!

Beck flew to the tearoom.

Dulcie the baking-talent fairy

was in a tizzy.

"Something has been nibbling

my carrot cake!"

Dulcie cried.

She pointed at the cake.

There was a huge chunk missing

from one side.

Beck clapped her hands together.

It had to be Bitty!

She looked around.

But she didn't find

the baby bunny.

She found Prilla

with icing on her lips

and a piece of cake in her hand.

"It tastes good!"

Prilla told Beck.

Beck's wings drooped.

She flew slowly

out of the tearoom.

She had looked everywhere.

There was no sign of Bitty.

Beck sighed.

She had no choice.

She had to ask Fawn for help.

Fawn would tease her.

But together they might

find the lost baby bunny.

Beck flew to where
she had seen Fawn
earlier in the day.
Fawn wasn't there.
But then Beck heard
a familiar sound.
Rustle, rustle, rustle.
The noise was coming
from a clump of clover.

41

She flew closer.

Rustle, rustle, rustle.

Beck parted the leaves

of the clover.

Inside was Fawn . . .

with Bitty!

"Fawn!" Beck cried.

Fawn jumped.

Her glow turned bright pink.

"Oh, Beck! I've been taking care

of this lost baby bunny,"

Fawn said.

"I didn't want to tell you

because I always tease you

for taking in baby animals."

Beck laughed and laughed.

Fawn put her hands on her hips.

"What's so funny?"

she asked.

"I was taking care
of the bunny, too,"
Beck said.
"So you see,
we kept Bitty a secret
from each other!"

Fawn laughed, too.

Beck and Fawn linked hands

over Bitty's soft fur.

"I have an idea," Beck said.

"From now on,

let's take care of Bitty

together!"